My First Book

A BABAR™ BABY JOURNAL

Abrams Books for Young Readers, New York

This book belongs to

Gabriel Roger Taylor

born on

March 14, 2009 @ 11:39 am

[Paste photo here]

My Mother's Family Tree

MOTHER

Name Angelina Taylor
Birth date September 6 1982
Birthplace Morehead City NC

GRANDMOTHER

Name Patty Benjamin
Birth date _____
Birthplace _____

GRANDFATHER

Name Rick Benjamin
Birth date _____
Birthplace _____

GRANDMOTHER'S MOTHER

Name _____
Birth date _____
Birthplace _____

GRANDFATHER'S MOTHER

Name _____
Birth date _____
Birthplace _____

GRANDMOTHER'S FATHER

Name _____
Birth date _____
Birthplace _____

GRANDFATHER'S FATHER

Name _____
Birth date _____
Birthplace _____

My Father's Family Tree

FATHER

Name _Casey Taylor_
Birth date _October 13, 1980_
Birthplace _Kalispell MT_

GRANDMOTHER

Name _Robbin Taylor_
Birth date _May 10, 1960_
Birthplace _____

GRANDFATHER

Name _Ron Taylor_
Birth date _April 4, 1958_
Birthplace _____

GRANDMOTHER'S MOTHER

Name _____
Birth date _____
Birthplace _____

GRANDFATHER'S MOTHER

Name _____
Birth date _____
Birthplace _____

GRANDMOTHER'S FATHER

Name _____
Birth date _____
Birthplace _____

GRANDFATHER'S FATHER

Name _____
Birth date _____
Birthplace _____

My Mother

Here is a photo of my mother:

My mother's full name is Angelina Catherine Taylor

She was born on Sept 6th 1982 in Morehead City NC

Her height is 5 6 , her eye color is brown , and her hair color is light brown

She has 0 sisters and 0 brothers and they were born in this order:

She grew up in North Carolina and went to these schools: Laney High school, Hoggard High School, East Carteret High School,

After school, she Drama Club went home hung out with friends. Practice for chorus

When my mother was a young woman, she dreamed of being a lawyer joining the Navy

These are some of my mother's favorite things:

artist David Mack, Amy Brown
book
color Pink
film 10 Things I hate about you. Diary of a mad Black Woman
flower Sunflowers
hobby Scrapbooking
holiday Christmas & Easter
place In hubbies arms. (Daddies)
game Legos Indiana Jones - board games, canasta
season Fall
song Hero -
sport Football - Cowboys!

These are some of the things that make my mother special:

_____

_____

_____

_____

_____

When my mother was a baby, she looked like this:

My Father

Here is a photo of my father:

My father's full name is _Casey Jason Taylor_

He was born on _Oct 13, 1980_ in _Kalispell MT_

His height is _5'7_ , his eye color is _Blue_ , and his hair color is _Red/Blonde_

He has _1_ sisters and _1_ brothers, and they were born in this order:
Luke Taylor   Clarissa Peterson

He grew up in ___Seatac WA___ and went to these schools:

_____

_____

After school, he _____

_____

_____

When my father was a young man, he dreamed of _____

_____

_____

These are some of my father's favorite things:

artist _____

book _____

color _____

film _____

flower _____

hobby _____

holiday _____

place _____

game _____

season _____

song _____

sport _____

These are some of the things that make my father special:

_____

_____

_____

_____

When my father was a baby, he looked like this:

14

My Parents' Courtship and Marriage

Here is a photo of my mother and father before they were married:

My parents met on <u>9/26/05</u> at <u>Food Lion Parking lot in Jacksonville NC</u>

My father's first impression of my mother was _____
_____
_____

My mother's first impression of my father was _wow, he looks much_
better in person.

The things they really like about each other are _____

My parents were married on _November 18, 2006_ at _the base chapel in_
Jacksonville NC

Here is a photo of my mother and father on their wedding day:

My Big Brothers and Sisters

These are my siblings' names and ages:

_____

_____

_____

_____

Here is a photo of my brothers and sisters:

My Maternal Grandparents

Here are photos of my mother's mother and father:

My Paternal Grandparents

Here are photos of my father's mother and father:

Waiting for Me to Arrive

My mother found out she was pregnant on July 1st 2008 @ 2:00 Am

Her reaction to the news was ummm baby... I think we are pregnant. We had been trying w/ no avail. So daddy and I both were shocked.

My father's reaction to the news was _____

The first people who heard about me were our parents - we woke both of them up

My mother's due date was March 6th 2009

My mother first heard my heartbeat on _____

She felt me kicking on _____

My father first heard my heartbeat on _____

He felt me kicking on _____

Before I was born, my parents liked to call me meatball

22

Here is a photo of me before I was born:

[Paste ultrasound photo here]

While pregnant with me, my mother craved chocolate, strawberry shakes McDonalds Fries, Twizzlers

And she no longer liked to eat - H No more starbucks

Here are some photos of my mother pregnant with me:

A Baby Shower

Robbin Taylor, Charissa, Sara _____ hosted a baby shower on March 1st, 2009

[Paste shower invitation here]

Guests	Gifts	Thank-You Note Sent

Here are some photos from the shower:

The Day I Was Born

My mother went into labor on ___Friday march 13, 2009___ at __4__ o'clock.

At the time, she and my father were __at Valley hospital__

The labor and delivery lasted __20   LONG hours__

I was born on __march 14, 2009__ at __11:39 am__ o'clock.

When my mother first saw me, she __was thankful he was healthy and finally here.__

_____
_____

When my father first saw me, he _____
_____
_____
_____

When my mother first held me, she _____
_____
_____
_____

When my father first held me, he _____
_____
_____
_____

When I was born, I weighed ___9lbs. .5oz___ and was ___20___ inches long.

14 3/4 inch head

I had ___blue___ eyes and ___Adarn___ hair.

Special things my mother and father noticed about me were ___beautiful blue___ ___eyes. Looked just like daddy. I was a big___ ___baby___

My mother thought I looked like ___Daddy___

My father thought I looked like _____

Other people said I looked like ___Daddy___

Here is my hospital bracelet:

Here are some photos of me right after I was born:

The Day My Mother and Father Adopted Me

I met my mother and father on _____
at _____

When my mother first saw me, she _____
_____
_____
_____

When my father first saw me, he _____
_____
_____
_____

When I came to live with my parents, I was _____ years old.

I had been living in _____

This is the story of my adoption _____
_____
_____
_____
_____
_____
_____
_____

_____

_____

_____

_____

_____

Here is the first photo my parents have of me:

Here are some photos of me with my parents on the day that we met:

My Name

My parents chose my name because Daddy chose your name. Gabriel is a very strong person in the Bible. Daddy really likes it. Roger is his paternal grandfathers name. Daddy was very close to him and misses him immensly. But knows he is watching over you, and very proud to have a grandson named after him.

The meaning of my name is Gabriel - Strong man of God

My nicknames are Gabe, meatball

Here are some of the other names my parents considered:

Boys' names	Girls' names
	Isabella
	Elisabeth

My Tiny Hands and Feet

Here is my little footprint:

[Paste footprint here]

Here is my sweet handprint:

[Paste handprint here]

My Birth Announcement

[Paste birth announcement here]

The World on the Day I Was Born

On the day I was born, the weather was _____

The president was _____

Some important local and national events were _____
_____
_____
_____

Some important world events were _____
_____
_____
_____

Favorite movie stars were _____
_____
_____

Hit movies and television shows were _____
_____
_____

Popular singers and songs were _____
_____
_____

Best-selling books were _____
_____
_____

Prominent sports figures were _____
_____
_____

Some fashion fads were _____
_____
_____

Some prices of things were _____
_____
_____

[Paste newspaper headlines here]

My Mother's Memories of My Birth and First Few Days

_____

_____

_____

_____

_____

_____

_____

_____

_____

_____

_____

_____

_____

_____

_____

_____

_____

_____

_____

_____

_____

_____

My Father's Memories of My Birth and First Few Days

My Mother's Hopes and Wishes for Me

_____
_____
_____
_____
_____
_____
_____
_____

Here is a photo of me with my mother:

My Father's Hopes and Wishes for Me

_____

_____

_____

_____

_____

_____

_____

Here is a photo of me with my father:

My Home Sweet Home

My mother and father brought me home on __Monday March 16th__ at __5__ o'clock.

At the time, my family lived at __2750-C Warner Ave Enumclaw WA 98022__

When we arrived, we were greeted by __Gramma - mommies mom__ _____

Here are some photos of my homecoming:

Here is a photo of where I live:

Here is a photo of my nursery:

My First Visitors

My first visitors were _____

_____

_____

_____

_____

_____

_____

_____

They thought I was _____

_____

_____

_____

_____

_____

_____

_____

_____

_____

_____

_____

_____

_____

_____

_____

Notes About My First Week at Home

Here are some photos of me during my first week at home:

Rock-a-Bye Baby!

Lullabies my mother and father sing to me are _____
_____

My sleeping schedule and habits are _____
_____
_____
_____

To help me fall asleep my mother and father _____
_____
_____
_____

The first time I slept through the night was _____

Here is a photo of me asleep:

Mealtime

I first ate solid food on _____

My favorite foods are _____
_____
_____

My least favorite foods are _____
_____
_____

I first held my own bottle on _____

I first fed myself on _____

Here is a photo of me eating:

Out on the Town

The date of my first outing was _____

I went to _____ with _____

I reacted by _____
_____
_____
_____
_____

Here is a photo of me on my first day out and about:

Rub-a-dub-dub!

I had my first bath on _____

I reacted by _____
_____
_____

Things I like about taking a bath are _____
_____
_____

Things I don't like about taking a bath are _____
_____
_____

Here is a photo of me in the tub:

My First Haircut

I had my first haircut on _____

I reacted by _____
_____
_____

Here is a lock of my hair:

My First Tooth

My first tooth appeared on _____

Some Other Firsts

I lifted my head up on _____

I rolled over on _____

I sat up by myself on _____

I crawled on _____

I pulled myself into a standing position on _____

I took my first step on _____

I walked from my mother to my father by myself on _____

I clapped my hands on _____

I waved bye-bye on _____

I played peekaboo on _____

Other physical firsts of note:

_____

_____

_____

_____

_____

_____

_____

_____

_____

_____

_____

_____

_____

_____

_____

_____

_____

_____

_____

_____

_____

_____

My Expressive Firsts

I first smiled on _____

I first laughed on _____

I first made cooing sounds on _____

I first imitated sounds on _____

I said my first word on _____

My first word was _____

My first phrase was _____

Other expressive firsts of note:

_____

_____

_____

_____

_____

_____

_____

_____

_____

_____

_____

_____

A Record of My First Words

Word   Date Spoken

_____|_____
_____|_____
_____|_____
_____|_____
_____|_____

These are some other funny things I said:

_____
_____
_____
_____
_____
_____
_____
_____
_____
_____

Happy Holidays!

My first holiday was _____

My family celebrated by _____

_____

_____

_____

_____

I wore _____

Here is a photo of me on my first holiday:

Other Holiday Photos

First Discoveries

When I first rode on a swing, I _____
_____

When I first went swimming, I _____
_____

When I first saw snow, I _____
_____

When I first heard thunder, I _____
_____

When I first ate ice cream, I _____
_____

When I first ate cake, I _____
_____

Other first discoveries:
_____
_____
_____
_____
_____
_____

Some of My Favorite Things

Activities _____

Animals _____

Bath toys _____

Books _____

Nursery rhymes _____

People _____

Songs _____

Stories _____

Stuffed animals _____

Television programs _____

Toys _____

Treats _____

Videos _____

These are some of my other favorite things:

_____

_____

_____

_____

_____

_____

_____

_____

_____

_____

_____

_____

_____

_____

_____

_____

_____

_____

_____

_____

_____

_____

Inching My Way Up!

Date	Age	Height	Weight

Visits to the Doctor

Date	Reason for Visit	Comments

A Record of My First Year

Here are some more of my first photos:

1st Month

2nd Month

3ʳᵈ Month

My Photos

4th Month

5th Month

6th Month

My Photos

7th Month

8th Month

9th Month

My Photos

10th Month

11th Month

My Photos

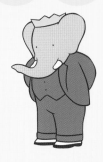

My First Birthday Party!

[Paste party invitation here]

We celebrated my first birthday by _____
_____

What I thought of the party, cake, and candles: _____
_____

Guests	Gifts

My Birthday Party Photos

Library of Congress Control Number: 2004104284
ISBN 13: 978-0-8109-4934-8
ISBN 10: 0-8109-4934-2

Conceived and developed by Harry N. Abrams, Incorporated, New York.
Images adapted by Peter Wolski, after characters created by Jean and Laurent de Brunhoff.
Text written by Sarah H. Kennedy.

Production Manager: Jonathan Lopes

Printed and bound in China
10 9 8 7 6 5 4 3 2

HNA
harry n. abrams, inc.
a subsidiary of La Martinière Groupe
115 West 18th Street
New York, NY 10011
www.hnabooks.com